ADAPTED FROM THE CLASSIC NOVEL BY EDGAR RICE BURROUGHS

TARZAN

RETOLD BY

ROBERT D. SAN SOUCI

ILLUSTRATED BY

MICHAEL McCURDY

HYPERION

BOOKS

FOR

CHILDREN

NEW YORK

In 1888, mutineers took control of the ship carrying Lord and Lady Greystoke to Africa. The young couple were abandoned on a lonely shore with some food and tools. While John Greystoke built them a cabin, Alice awaited the birth of their first child. But soon after the baby boy arrived, Lady Greystoke died. . . .

In the forest lived a tribe of great apes, ruled by cruel, foul-tempered Kerchak. One day Kerchak, followed by two males, approached the curious nest where strange white apes lived. Behind came Kala, a young female. Before, the apes had been driven off by the thunder-stick the male carried. It always roared out death for a member of the tribe. But though the door was open, the white ape did not appear with the stick.

Kerchak peered in. The strange male sat weeping beside a bed on which the female lay dead. From a cradle came the wail of a babe.

John Greystroke barely had a chance to look up before Kerchak attacked and finished him. Then the ape turned to the cradle—but Kala snatched the baby and fled to a high tree. There she quieted and tended the tiny child.

Kerchak started to follow her, but then he spotted the thunder-stick. The child forgotten, he turned the stick this way and that. It fired! KERCHOOM! Terrified, the apes fled. In their clumsy haste the door closed, and the sturdy latch dropped into place.

In the years that followed, Kala protected her foster child from Kerchak's rages and the jungle's other dangers. By the age of ten—when great apes were fully grown—Kala's charge was still a boy. But he was clever and intelligent. He was strong, too, and could speed from branch to branch.

But he was unhappy because he was different. When he saw his reflection in a pool, he felt ugly compared to his hairy fellows. The tribe called him "Tarzan," meaning "white skin."

He was also unlike the apes in his eagerness to learn. When the tribe wandered near the sealed cabin, his companions ignored the place as they hunted for food, roughhoused, groomed themselves, or slept. But Tarzan would pat and poke and pry at the walls and roof for hours, seeking a way in. At last he figured out how to undo the latch.

He ignored the two skeletons as he explored. His best discovery was a hunting knife. He cut his fingers several times before he learned to hold it properly. Just as exciting were books filled with colorful pictures. For hours he looked at the pictures and the letters—he thought them "bugs"—under them. Some drawings were things he knew: Sabor, the lioness; Tantor, the elephant; and Bara, the deer. Others were baffling, for he had never seen such things.

When he left, he latched the door, taking only the knife to show his fellows. Suddenly, Bolgani the gorilla charged at him from the green shadows. Recalling how the knife had hurt him, Tarzan thrust it at his giant enemy. The wounded gorilla fought fiercely, but Tarzan finally slew him.

All the other apes were amazed by this feat— and more so by the knife Tarzan carried everywhere. Even Kerchak eyed him with respect.

Returning often to the cabin, Tarzan learned the secret of the "bugs" on each page. By age fifteen, he recognized the words that went with each picture. When he found some pencils he copied the "bugs" and so began to write.

He no longer felt shamed by his hairless body or different features, for now he understood that he was of another race. He was H-U-M-A-N; his companions were A-P-E-S. He knew that Sabor was a L-I-O-N-E-S-S; Tantor, an E-L-E-P-H-A-N-T; and Bara, a D-E-E-R. And so he learned to read.

But he was still part of the tribe. One night he joined in a Dum-Dum ceremony to celebrate the victory of Kerchak's tribe over enemy apes that had invaded their territory. While the females beat on a huge mound of earth with knotted branches, the males danced and roared beneath the rising moon.

Suddenly Kerchak was seized with madness and rage. His fury turned upon Tarzan, who danced like a great ape, but whose hairless skin gleamed in the moonlight. With a screech, Kerchak launched himself at Tarzan. The drumming stopped; the other apes froze. Tarzan, his knife at the ready, faced the king.

Kala, his foster mother, leaped snarling at Kerchak. But the huge male knocked her aside. Then Tarzan charged. His blade cut Kerchak's arm. Making a noisy show of defiance, the old ape king backed away.

Tarzan helped Kala to her feet. Raising his eyes to the full moon, he voiced the blood-chilling cry of the great apes. Staring into Kerchak's wicked red eyes, he shouted, "I am Tarzan. I am a great fighter. Let all respect Tarzan of the Apes and Kala, his mother. There is none among you as mighty as Tarzan. Let his enemies beware."

Kerchak thumped his chest and shrilled his own cry. Then he turned away. But the tribe sensed that someday the two would meet in deadly combat.

In the days that followed, Tarzan grew stronger and wiser, and learned many amazing things from his books. Beyond the J-U-N-G-L-E or across the O-C-E-A-N, many H-U-M-A-N-S lived in a C-I-T-Y, a place of strange nests as big as mountains.

He carefully studied pictures of wrestlers and swimmers, and learned their skills. Guided by the books, he fashioned a bow and arrows, a loincloth, and a sheath for his knife.

One day Kala, grown old and careless, was so busy digging grubs from a tree stump she did not notice Sabor, the lioness, stalking her. Too late, Kala drew herself up and faced her enemy with a bellow. A moment later she fell to Sabor's paw.

Tarzan, answering Kala's cry, found the lioness crouched over the body of his foster mother. His grief and anger were unbounded. He roared out his challenge and beat his fists on his great chest. He fitted an arrow to his bowstring and boldly dropped to the ground, not twenty paces from Sabor.

The lioness's great yellow eyes fixed upon the ape-man with a wicked gleam, and her red tongue licked her lips. She tensed, ready to spring. But when she leaped, Tarzan's arrow caught her in midair. At the same instant Tarzan jumped to one side. As the great cat struck the ground beyond him, another arrow sank deep into her side.

With a mighty roar the beast turned and charged once more, only to be met with a deadly third arrow; but this time she was too close for the ape-man to sidestep her. Tarzan of the Apes went down beneath the great body of his enemy. He lay stunned for a moment, before he realized that Sabor was dead.

Later, seated upon a broad tree limb, Tarzan proudly showed Sabor's skin to the great apes. "Look! Apes of Kerchak," he cried, "see what Tarzan the mighty hunter has done. He has slain the killer of his mother, Kala. Tarzan is mightiest among you for Tarzan is no ape. Tarzan is—"

He stopped, because the apes had no word for *human*; and Tarzan could only write the word, he could not say it.

The tribe had gathered to listen. Only Kerchak held back. Suddenly, something snapped in the ape. With a frightful cry, the huge beast sprang at Tarzan, who was just out of reach.

"Come down, Tarzan, great killer," Kerchak taunted. "Come down and feel my fangs. Mighty fighters do not hide in trees."

As the other apes watched, Tarzan leaped down and faced the leader, his knife drawn. The struggle was fierce, though Tarzan's knife helped balance Kerchak's greater bulk and strength.

Then Kerchak smashed Tarzan's knife hand, sending his weapon spinning. But the ape-man managed to get behind Kerchak. Using a wrestling hold learned from one of his books, Tarzan locked an arm across Kerchak's throat, then tightened his grip. It was now in his power to break his enemy's neck. Reason kept him from doing so.

If I kill him, thought Tarzan, it will rob the tribe of a great fighter. If he is alive, he will always be an example of my power to the other apes.

"*Ka-goda?*" hissed Tarzan. "Do you surrender?"

Kerchak growled and struggled harder. Tarzan added pressure, which forced a grunt of pain from the beast.

"*Ka-goda!*" cried Kerchak, defeated.

Tarzan relaxed his hold. "I am Tarzan, King of the Apes, mighty hunter, mighty fighter. In all the jungle there is none so great. You have said *Ka-goda* to me. All the tribe heard. I am king now. Do you understand?"

But when Tarzan released him, the ape turned upon him. As they struggled, it seemed that Kerchak was winning. But Tarzan once again used his wits as well as his strength to catch Kerchak in a death grip. This time, the new king of the apes showed his treacherous subject no mercy. Nor did Kerchak seek it—snarling and snapping and scratching at his captor. Tarzan jerked his arm suddenly. Kerchak shuddered, then his body stiffened; a moment later, he sank lifeless to the ground. The harsh justice of the jungle had been served.

So Tarzan became the undisputed ruler of the apes. But he soon tired of kingship. It left him little time to visit the cabin and study his books. He was growing further apart from the apes, who had no interest in such things and who were impatient to move into the deep forest.

One dawn Tarzan called the tribe together. "Tarzan is not an ape," he said. "His ways are not your ways. Tarzan goes to seek his true tribe. You must choose a new king, for Tarzan will not return."

So saying, the ape-man strode boldly into the breaking day and toward his destiny.

AUTHOR'S NOTE

When I was in fourth grade, I first discovered the books of Edgar Rice Burroughs. I was enthralled by the adventures of John Carter of Mars, Carson of Venus, Tanar of Pellucidar (at the center of the earth), and, of course, Tarzan. I would ask for the books as gifts, and I would comb used bookstores to buy the sequels to the original *Tarzan of the Apes*, using money I earned mowing lawns. There was nothing more wonderful than a fresh Tarzan novel—how I savored each thrilling moment!

Tarzan has called countless readers to armchair adventures before and since. James Cawthorn and Michael Moorcock, writing in *Fantasy: The 100 Best Books*, call the ape-man "the world's best-selling fictional hero"—the remarkable creation of a remarkable writer.

TARZAN OF THE APES

Tarzan of the Apes first appeared as a short story in 1912. Burroughs expanded the work and published it as a book in 1914. It was followed by twenty-two sequels. Although the series has faults—the author's dialogue can be awkward and his plots are often similar and rely heavily on coincidence—Burroughs has a genuine talent for writing exciting action scenes. He creates suspense that keeps readers eagerly turning pages and brings alive remarkable heroes and memorable villains.

One of his greatest gifts is that of world-building: he details the histories, peoples, creatures, cities, languages, customs, artwork, games, and clothing of imaginary places so carefully that they ring true. Tarzan's fantasy jungle has become real to generations of readers.

Condensing the novel to picture-book length involved selecting the key moments that give a coherent presentation of Tarzan's origins, his rise to king of the tribe of great apes, and his growing appreciation of the intelligence and reason that separate him from the primates. One of the most interesting (and most debated) plot elements concerns how Tarzan learns to read. As a young reader, I was intrigued by the idea that one could unlock the secrets in books without outside guidance. I think the concept offers a basis for fruitful discussion—as well as a subtle reinforcement of the importance of reading for everyone.

Tarzan's Africa is largely imaginary: Burroughs never visited the continent. When a critic pointed out that *Tarzan of the Apes* included a tiger (not found in Africa), Burroughs quickly corrected this error. The comparatively intelligent "great apes," who have a rudimentary language, and who adopt Tarzan, are also fictions. They are unlike any existing species; and primates cannot speak because their throats do not allow them to form words.

Presumably Mowgli, the boy reared by wolves in Rudyard Kipling's *The Jungle Book*, inspired Burroughs's concept of an ape-man. And Burroughs probably was aware of newspaper and magazine accounts of "wild children" such as a gazelle-boy or a wolf-girl raised by creatures of the wild. The idea of an animal as foster parent to abandoned children goes back to such ancient tales as the story of the orphaned Romulus and Remus, the founders of Rome, who were tended by a she-wolf. A number of studies indicate there may be truth in some of the better-documented cases.

The jungle lord of the books is far more interesting than the one found in movies or on television. Tarzan is a hero torn between his upbringing (as a child of the jungle) and his heritage (as child of the civilized world). By the time he becomes ruler of the apes, he is growing apart from them, prompted by his superior brain, and drawn to the wonders of civilization, which he discovers in books in his parents' cabin.

Tarzan represents philosopher Jean-Jacques Rousseau's ideal of the "noble savage": a person who grows up virtuous and wise in the natural world, untouched and uncorrupted by cultured society. And Tarzan belongs in the company of heroes from Gilgamesh and Hercules to Sir Lancelot and Luke Skywalker.

The heroes of legend were often born of one mortal and one divine parent; Tarzan's parents come from what seems at first an almost divine or magical place—the civilized world. Heroes are often abandoned as children, or raised by foster parents; orphaned Tarzan is cared for by Kala the ape.

Heroes are endowed with great courage and strength, and are celebrated for their brave deeds; Tarzan embodies all this. Heroes undertake great quests, often to seek their birthright. On the journey, heroes gain wisdom and self-understanding. Tarzan, also, is on a quest to reclaim his heritage as a child of the civilized world; his adventures and discoveries bring him newfound wisdom and insight.

In sum, Tarzan fits the classic pattern of the hero or heroine on a quest for knowledge and fulfillment of a destiny he or she may only partly understand when starting out. This timeless subtext, undergirding Edgar Rice Burroughs's gift for storytelling, helps explain why Tarzan is one of the most enduring figures in popular literature.

For information address Hyperion Books for Children,
114 Fifth Avenue, New York, New York 10011-5690.
First Edition
1 3 5 7 9 8 6 4 2

Printed in the United States of America.

Text for this book is set in 20-point Celestia Antigua.
Artwork was prepared using scratchboard prints and colored pencils.
Designed by Christine Kettner.

LIBRARY OF CONGRESS CATALOGING-IN-PUBLICATION DATA
San Souci, Robert D.
Tarzan/retold by Robert D. San Souci; illustrated by Michael McCurdy.—1st ed.
p. cm.
Summary: A baby boy, left alone in the African jungle after the death of his parents,
is adopted by an ape and raised to manhood without ever seeing another human being.
ISBN 0-7868-0384-3 (trade: alk. paper).—ISBN 0-7868-2334-8 (lib.: alk. paper)
[1. Feral children—Fiction. 2. Apes—Fiction. 3. Jungles—Fiction. 4. Africa—Fiction.] I. McCurdy,
Michael, ill. II. Burroughs, Edgar Rice, 1875–1950. Tarzan. III. Title.
PZ7.S1947Tar 1999
[Fic]—dc21 98-39041

Northport-East Northport Public Library

To view your patron record from a computer, click on
the Library's homepage: **www.nenpl.org**

You may:
- request an item be placed on hold
- renew an item that is overdue
- view titles and due dates checked out on your card
- view your own outstanding fines

151 Laurel Avenue
Northport, NY 11768
631-261-6930